D1132923

398.2
Sin
c.3

Singer, Isaac Bashevis
Mazel and Shlimazel

Date Due

KLA.R	2 28 '75	
WIL C A4	6—'79	
MONTA D 9 / 13 '79		
BUTTE A 5	15 '83	
DORR	4 27 '86	

Siskiyou County Schools Library
E.S.E.A. TITLE II, PHASE TWO, 1969

Mazel, good luck, and Shlimazel, bad luck, make a bet one day. Whatever good Mazel can do, in a year, Shlimazel will undo in a second and win a barrel of wine of forgetfulness. Mazel helps Tam, an impoverished boy, gain the confidence of the King and the love of the Princess. But when Tam gets some lioness' milk to cure the ailing King, Shlimazel takes control of Tam's tongue when he presents the milk and it seems that Shlimazel has won. However, Shlimazel, drunk with the wine, forgets Tam, and Mazel, again, offers help.

21163

MAZEL AND SHLIMAZEL

ISAAC BASHEVIS SINGER

MAZEL AND SHLIMAZEL

OR THE MILK OF A LIONESS

PICTURES BY MARGOT ZEMACH

Translated from the Yiddish by the author and Elizabeth Shub

FARRAR, STRAUS & GIROUX, NEW YORK

· *An Ariel Book* ·

Siskiyou County Schools Library
E.S.E.A. TITLE II, PHASE TWO, 1969

Text © 1967 Isaac Bashevis Singer. Pictures © 1967 Margot Zemach. All rights reserved.
L.C. catalog card 67–19887. Published simultaneously in Canada by Ambassador Books,
Ltd., Rexdale, Ontario. Printed in the United States of America. Designed by Atha Tehon

IN a faraway land, on a sunny spring day, the sky was as blue as the sea, and the sea was as blue as the sky, and the earth was green and in love with them both. Two spirits were passing through a village. One was called Mazel, which means good luck, and the other, Shlimazel, bad luck.

Spirits are not seen by man, but they can see one another.

Mazel was young, tall, slim. His cheeks were pink and he had sand-colored hair. He was dressed in a green jacket, red riding breeches, and wore a hat with a feather in it. There were silver spurs on his high boots. Mazel seldom walked. Usually he rode his horse, which was also a spirit. On this particular day, he felt like strolling through the village on foot.

I

Siskiyou County Schools Library
E.S.E.A. TITLE II, PHASE TWO, 1969

Shlimazel limped along beside him with the help of a knotty-wood cane—an old man with a wan face and angry eyes under his bushy brows. His nose was crooked and red from drinking. His beard was as gray as spider webs. He was attired in a long black coat and on his head sat a peaked hat.

Mazel spoke and Shlimazel listened. Mazel was in a boasting mood. "Everybody wants me, everybody loves me," he said. "Wherever I go, I bring joy. Naturally the people cannot see me because I am a spirit, but they all long for me just the same: merchants and sailors, doctors and shoemakers, lovers and card players. All over the world they call, 'Mazel come to me.' Nobody calls for you, Shlimazel. You'll have to admit that what I say is true."

Shlimazel pursed his lips and clutched his beard. "Yes, I must agree that you're a charmer," he said. "But the world is ruled by the strong and not by the charming. What can take you a year to accomplish, I can destroy in one second."

Shlimazel had made a point and now Mazel bit his lip in annoyance. "We all know you can destroy," he replied. "But you always do it in the same way—either you kill, or you burn, or you send sickness or famine, war or poverty. I, on the other hand, am always full of fresh ideas. I know millions of ways to make people happy."

"I have billions of ways of making them unhappy."

"That's not true. You always use the same old tricks," Mazel insisted. "I'll bet that you can't even find a single new way of spoiling something nice that I've done."

"Is that so? What will you wager?" Shlimazel countered.

"If you win," Mazel said, "I will give you a barrel of the precious wine of forgetfulness. If you lose, you keep your red nose out of my business for fifty years."

"Agreed," Shlimazel replied. "Well, what will you do that's so nice?"

"I will go to the poorest hut in this village and bring happiness to whoever lives there. I will remain with that person for an entire year. The moment the year is at an end, you may take over, but only on condition that you will neither kill him through a mishap nor make him sick nor impoverish him. And on no account are you to use any of your old and tired games. Now, how much time will you need to undo what I will have done?"

"One second," Shlimazel replied.

"It's a bet."

Mazel stretched out his hand. The green gem of hope sparkled from a ring on his third finger. He grasped Shlimazel's gaunt and wrinkled hand, which had crooked fingers with horny nails. The day was warm, but Shlimazel's hand was as cold as ice.

Soon after they parted, Mazel came to a hut which he knew must be the poorest in the village. The logs from which it had

been built were rotted and covered with moss. Its thatched roof had turned black with time. There was no chimney and the smoke from the stove escaped through a hole in the roof. The glass panes had long since disappeared from the windows, which were boarded over.

Mazel had to bend his head to get through the door. Inside, toadstools sprouted from the unplastered walls.

On a broken-down cot which was covered with straw sat a young peasant lad. He was barefoot and half naked. Mazel asked him his name.

"Tam," he replied.

"Why are you so down and out?" Mazel inquired.

Tam could not see Mazel, but nevertheless he spoke to him, thinking that he was talking to himself. Tam said: "I once had parents, but they were unlucky. My father died of consumption.

My mother went to the forest to gather mushrooms and was bitten by a poisonous snake. The small piece of land they left me is so full of rocks that I can hardly farm it. And last year there was a drought and a locust plague. This year I won't even have a harvest because I had nothing to sow."

"Still, one shouldn't lose hope," Mazel said.

"What can I hope for?" Tam asked. "If you don't sow, you don't reap. My clothes are in tatters and the girls of the village laugh at me. A man without luck is worse than dead."

"Something good may still happen," suggested Mazel.

"When?"

"Soon."

"How?"

Before Mazel could reply, there was a sound of trumpets and galloping hooves. Twenty-four royal guards on horseback preceded the king's carriage drawn by six white stallions. The horsemen were uniformed in red pantaloons, yellow tunics, and plumed white helmets. A company of courtiers, also mounted, followed the carriage.

All the villagers had come out to admire the royal travelers. Whoever was wearing a hat removed it. Some of the villagers kneeled. The girls curtsied.

At first it looked as if the carriage would pass through the village without stopping and the people would hardly be able to catch a glimpse of their king. But Mazel had already figured things out. As the carriage reached Tam's hut, one of its wheels rolled off, and the vehicle almost turned over. The riders reined in their horses and the entire company came to a standstill.

The door of the carriage opened and the king came out, followed by the seventeen-year-old Crown Princess Nesika, his only child. Nesika was famous for her beauty both at home and abroad. The royal party was returning from a ball given in her honor by the king of a neighboring land. The princess's golden hair fell to her shoulders, her eyes were blue, her skin white, her neck long, and her waist narrow. She was gowned in a white dress reaching to the tips of her slippers. The king had always spoiled her because her mother had died when Nesika was small. But today he was angry at his lovely daughter.

The purpose of the ball had been to introduce Nesika to Crown Prince Typpish and a match was to be arranged between them. However, Nesika had not liked the prince, and he was the seventh prince in a row that she had rejected. Of the first, she had said that he laughed too loud and too often. The second spoke of nothing but his skill at hunting foxes. She had seen the third beating his dog. The fourth had the most irritating habit of beginning each sentence with "I." The fifth had been a practical joker. The sixth had the habit of telling the same stories over and over again. As for Typpish, Nesika had simply announced that she would not have him because his boots were foolish.

"How can boots be foolish?" her father asked.

"If the feet are foolish, the boots are foolish," Nesika replied.

"How can feet be foolish?" her father insisted.

"If the head is foolish, the feet are foolish," Nesika retorted.

Each time Nesika had found a reason not to be married. The king was beginning to be afraid she would turn into an old maid.

According to the law of the land, Nesika could only become queen on her father's death if she had a husband to help her rule. If she failed to marry, the prime minister, whose name was Kamtsan, would ascend the throne in her place. Kamtsan was well known for being an intriguer, a coward, and a miser. He was so extremely stingy that for their golden wedding anniversary, when it is customary to present an object of gold, he gave his beloved wife a tin thimble wrapped in gold paper.

When the wheel fell off his carriage, the already angry king flew into a rage. He rebuked his attendants for endangering his life and demanded to know which one of them could set the wheel back in place the fastest.

Tam knew little about fixing a wheel and nothing about fancy carriages. But since Mazel stood behind him, he was filled with courage and called out, "I can do it, Your Majesty."

The king looked with curiosity at the half-naked lad. After some hesitation, and a nudge from Mazel, he said: "If you can do it—do it—and quickly."

The villagers, who knew Tam as a ne'er-do-well and a bungler, watched in fear. They were sure that he would fail and that the king would vent his anger on the entire village.

WHEN Mazel stands behind a man, that man succeeds in everything, and so it was with Tam. As a young boy he had worked for a short time in a smithy, but he was sure that he remembered nothing of what he had learned there. However, no sooner had he picked up the wheel than everything came back to him. The king looked on in amazement at how deftly the young lad worked. When the job was finished, the king asked Tam how it happened that such an able young man was going around in tatters and lived in a ruin?

"Because I'm unlucky," Tam replied.

"Luck sometimes changes very quickly," the king said. "Come along to court, and we'll find something there for you to do."

It all happened so suddenly that the villagers could not believe their eyes. The king simply opened the door of his carriage and told Tam to get in. Then he gave the command to drive on.

Tam was in constant fear that the wheel would come off again, but even though the horses galloped along at full speed, the wheel remained in place.

The king and Nesika questioned Tam about his life in the village. The lad replied in a humble manner and his answers were brief and clever. Mazel was talking through him. The king turned to Nesika and spoke in a foreign language which Tam didn't understand, but Mazel did. "See what bright young men there are among our peasants." And Nesika replied in the same language: "Many a prince could learn from him." After a while she added thoughtfully: "He is handsome too. All he needs are some decent clothes."

Since Mazel had only a year's time to work in, things began to happen at once. That very day, as soon as they arrived at the palace, the king gave orders that a bath be prepared for Tam and he be given fresh linen and new clothes. He was put to work in the royal smithy.

Tam very soon began to show unusual skill. He could mend carriages that were considered beyond repair. He could shoe horses so wild that no one else dared go near them. He also turned out to be a great horseman. In less than a month he was appointed master of the king's stables.

Once each year the royal races were held at court. Tam was permitted to take part and he managed almost immediately to enchant the courtiers, visiting dignitaries, the king's wise men, and, as a matter of fact, the entire country.

Tam had chosen to ride an unknown horse, but with Mazel's help it became the fleetest horse in the history of the land. With Tam as rider it easily cleared the broadest ditches, the highest fences, and won all the purses. He cut such an elegant figure that all the ladies of the court fell in love with him.

Needless to say, Nesika had been in love with him from the very start. As always with those who are deeply in love, Nesika thought that her feelings for Tam were her secret. Actually, the entire court knew about it, even her father, the king. He also knew that lovers can be very stubborn. And since the proud king did not want to marry his daughter to the son of peasants, he decided to give Tam a task so challenging that he was bound to fail. He sent him with a small group of retainers into the depths of the kingdom to demand the allegiance of a wild and rebellious tribe that no lord of the king had been able to win over. With Mazel's help Tam not only succeeded but returned with magnificent gifts for the king and Princess Nesika.

Tam's fame continued to grow. Bards and minstrels sang of his deeds. High officials came to him for advice. He became the most admired and best-loved man in the kingdom. When the humble achieve success, they often become haughty and forget those among whom they grew up. Tam always found time to help the peasants and the poor.

It is known that the greater a man becomes, the more powerful are his enemies. Prime Minister Kamtsan, who wanted the throne, intrigued against Tam. He and his henchmen spread the word that Tam was a sorcerer. How else could a lowly peasant have managed to succeed where lords had failed? They said Tam had sold his soul to the devil. When that year, night after night, a strange comet with a long tail was seen in the sky, Tam's enemies insisted it was an omen that Tam would bring a misfortune on the king and lead the country to ruin.

SHLIMAZEL had promised Mazel to leave Tam in peace for a full year, but this did not prevent him from quietly preparing to trap Tam the moment the time was up. Shlimazel could not wait to win his bet and get hold of the barrel of the wine of forgetfulness. It was known that one sip of this wine gave more enjoyment than all other pleasurable things on earth. Shlimazel had for ages been suffering from sleeplessness and nightmares. He knew that the wine of forgetfulness would at last bring him sleep and sweet dreams of silver seas, golden rivers, gardens of crystal trees, and women of heavenly beauty. He also wanted to show his followers, the demons, goblins, hobgoblins, imps, and other evil spirits, that he was more powerful than Mazel and could outwit him.

Suddenly the king became ill. There were great doctors in the court but they could not discover what was wrong with him. At last, after long consultation, they decided that the king suffered from a rare disease for which the only cure was the milk of a lioness. Where does one get the milk of a lioness? There was a zoo in the capital, but at that moment it had no lioness with nursing cubs. The king's faith in Tam was so great that he sent for him and asked him to fetch the milk of a lioness. Anyone else in Tam's place would have been frightened out of his wits on hearing such a request. Since Mazel stood behind him, Tam replied simply: "Yes, my king, I will find a lioness, milk her, and bring her milk to you."

The king was so touched by Tam's brave reply that he called out to his courtiers: "You are my witnesses. The day Tam returns with the milk of a lioness, I will give him the hand of my daughter in marriage."

Prime Minister Kamtsan, standing among the courtiers, could contain himself no longer. "Your Majesty," he said, "no man can milk a lioness and live. Tam has made a promise that he cannot keep."

"And if he does bring milk, what guarantee is there that it will really be a lioness's milk?" added one of Kamtsan's followers.

"Your Majesty, I will find a lioness and milk her," Tam repeated with confidence.

"Go, and success be with you," the king said. "But I warn you: do not fool me by bringing me the milk of any other animal."

"If I deceive Your Majesty, I will deserve to die," Tam replied.

Everybody expected that Tam would arm himself with weapons and a net with which to ensnare the beast, or perhaps take along herbs with which to put the lioness to sleep. They could not believe he would travel without servants to help him. But he left alone and unarmed, riding his horse and carrying only a stone jug for the milk.

When the courtiers saw this, even those who had had confidence in Tam began to doubt. He had departed in such haste that he had not even stopped to bid farewell to anxious Nesika. Kamtsan's friends immediately spread the rumor that Tam had been so frightened by the difficult mission given him by the king that he had simply run away. All the wise men agreed that no lioness would let herself be milked by a human.

Of course, what nobody knew was that Mazel cantered along beside Tam. Tam had hardly ridden an hour's time when on a low hill he saw a large lioness. Her two cubs were standing nearby.

With the courage of those who are protected by Mazel, Tam approached the lioness, knelt down, and began to milk her as if she were a cow. He filled the jug with the lioness's warm milk, sealed it carefully, rose, and patted her on the head. Only then did the lioness seem to realize what had happened. Her yellow eyes seemed to say: "What have I permitted! Have I forgotten that I am queen of all the beasts? Where is my pride? My dignity?" And suddenly she let out a terrible roar. Luckily, Tam had already mounted his horse, for it bolted in fear and raced away in the direction of the capital.

When Tam returned so soon, everyone was convinced that the milk he brought back could not be that of a lioness. Lions lived in the desert, in a part of the kingdom that lay weeks away from the capital. It was clear to all that Tam intended to deceive the sick king so that when the king died Tam would rule through Nesika.

The king himself was as suspicious as the rest. Nevertheless, he summoned Tam to appear before him. Tam entered the royal chamber carrying the jug of milk in both hands.

Kneeling before the king, he said: "Your Majesty, I have brought what you sent me for—the milk of a dog."

A dead silence followed his words. The king's eyes filled with anger.

"You dare laugh at my misfortune. Milk of a dog you have brought me. You will pay for this with your life."

Why had Tam said that he had brought the milk of a dog?

It so happened that the very second that Tam approached the king's sickbed Mazel's year had come to an end and Shlimazel had taken his place. It was Shlimazel who made Tam say "dog" instead of "lioness."

Shlimazel had indeed in one second destroyed what had taken Mazel a year to do. And, as had been agreed between them, Shlimazel had not used any of his old tricks.

Tam tried to correct his mistake, but his voice was gone with his luck and he stood there speechless. At the king's signal, Kamtsan ordered two guards to seize Tam and place him in chains. They brought him to the dungeon where those condemned to death were kept.

When Nesika heard what had happened, she fell into despair. She ran to her father's chambers to beg him to save Tam. For the first time, the sick king refused to permit her into his presence.

THAT night the palace, indeed the whole capital, was dark and quiet. Only Kamtsan and his henchmen secretly celebrated Tam's downfall. They knew the king would soon die, and since Nesika was unmarried, Kamtsan would inherit the kingdom. The prime minister offered his guests bread and beer. Miser that he was, it was his custom to make his guests pay for their food and drink. On this occasion, however, he charged them only for their beer.

And in the deepest cellar of the palace, which was known to be haunted, Mazel and Shlimazel held their meeting. Shlimazel had expected Mazel to look disappointed and angry as do those who have lost a bet. But Mazel was not a sore loser. As usual, he was calm and composed.

"Shlimazel, you've won, and I congratulate you," he said.

"Do you realize that your lucky Tam will be hanged at dawn?" Shlimazel asked.

"Yes, I do."

"Have you forgotten my wine of forgetfulness?"

"No, I haven't."

Mazel went out and soon returned rolling a barrel covered with dust and cobwebs. He set it upright, handed Shlimazel a goblet, and said: "Drink, Shlimazel, as much as your heart desires." Shlimazel placed his goblet under the spigot, filled it, and drank greedily. A broad smirk spread over his devilish face. "For one who is the master of the unlucky," he grinned, "I sure am lucky."

He took another long drink, and, beginning to sound tipsy, he said, "Listen to me, Mazel. Instead of fighting me, why don't you join me? Together we'd make a great team."

Siskiyou County Schools Library
E.S.E.A. TITLE II, PHASE TWO, 1969

"You mean together we could ruin the world," Mazel said.

"Absolutely."

"And what then? After a while we'd have nothing left to do."

"As long as we can drink the wine of forgetfulness, why worry?"

"To get wine, someone has to plant the vineyard," Mazel reminded him. "Someone has to pick the grapes, press them, and prepare the wine. Nothing produces nothing—not even the wine of forgetfulness."

"If this wine works, I don't care about the future."

"It will work soon," Mazel said. "Drink and forget yourself."

"Have a drink, too, Mazel my friend."

"No, Shlimazel, forgetfulness is not for me."

Shlimazel drank one goblet after another. His wrinkled face half laughed, half cried, and he began to speak about himself in the way drunkards sometimes do.

"I wasn't born Shlimazel," he said. "My father was poor, but he was a good spirit. He was a water carrier in Paradise. My mother was a servant of a saint. My parents sent me to Reb Zeinvel's school. They wanted me to become a seraph or at least an angel. But I hated my parents because they forced me to study. To spite them, I joined a gang of imps. We did all kinds of mischief. We stole manna. We stuffed ourselves with pilfered star dust, moon milk, and other forbidden delicacies. At night we descended to earth, got into stables, and frightened horses.

32

We broke into larders and left devil's dung in the food. We disguised ourselves as wolves and chased sheep. What didn't we do? Once I turned myself into a frog and hid in Reb Zeinvel's snuffbox. When he opened it to take a pinch, I jumped out and bit his nose. I rose slowly but steadily in the ranks of the Evil Host until

I became what I am today—Shlimazel, Master of Bad Luck."
Shlimazel filled another goblet and began to sing in a hoarse voice:

You may plot and you may scheme,
Mazel is an empty dream.
Now Shlimazel's taken over,
Tam will never be in clover.
Mazel talks, Shlimazel acts,
Turning curses into facts.
Mazel wins a round or two,
Shlimazel sees the battle through.
On Mazel no one can depend,
Shlimazel's victor in the end.

Shlimazel uttered a snort and fell down like a log.

That was what Mazel had been waiting for. There was little time, because dawn was approaching and in the palace courtyard the dignitaries were already gathering for Tam's hanging. The guards appeared with Tam in chains. Kamtsan, surrounded by his flatterers, was conspicuous among the lords. He had already taken bribes and promised the highest positions to those who paid the most.

At a signal from Kamtsan, the drummers began their drumming. The masked executioner, dressed half in red and half in black, prepared to place the noose around Tam's neck. At that moment Mazel appeared. No one saw him but everybody felt his presence. The sun suddenly rose and covered everything with a purple light.

Now that Shlimazel lay in a drunken stupor and Mazel stood near the prisoner, Tam was again filled with courage. He called out in a clear voice: "My lords, it is the custom, before the condemned dies, to give him one last wish. My wish is to see the king."

The drummers, in confusion, interrupted their drumming. Though Kamtsan protested, the other lords overruled him and commanded that Tam be led to the king, who lay on his sickbed.

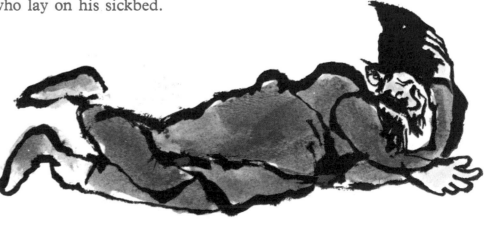

Tam knelt before the king and spoke: "Your Majesty, allow me to explain why I said that I had brought you the milk of a dog. It is known that the lion is the king of the animals, yet in comparison with you, My Lord, a lion is no more than a dog. And so I called the lioness a dog as an expression of my respect and admiration for Your Majesty. I did bring you the milk of a lioness. I beg you, drink it and it will make you well. I swear on my love for Nesika that I am telling the truth."

Since Mazel again stood at Tam's side, the king believed Tam. "But the milk has been poured out," Kamtsan interrupted.

Nesika, who had not slept all night, praying and hoping that Tam would somehow be saved, had heard what had taken place and had rushed to her father's room. When Kamtsan said that the milk had been thrown away, she cried out: "No, Kamtsan, I have kept it. I requested the servants to give it to me because I believed in Tam."

She ran herself to bring the milk to her father. The amazement of all present grew as they watched the king drink the milk to the last drop. It worked so quickly that he became well before their very eyes. His cheeks lost their pallor, his dim eyes regained their former brightness, and his strength returned. The entire court rejoiced, except, naturally, Kamtsan and those to whom he had sold high positions in the kingdom. Nesika was the happiest of all.

She fell at her father's feet and said: "Father, Tam saved your life. Every word he spoke was true. Now keep your promise and let us be married."

The king immediately ordered that a wedding be prepared fit for a future queen. Royalty and dignitaries were invited from all the surrounding countries. Kings, queens, princes, and princesses came to the wedding accompanied by their royal entourages. They brought the most precious gifts.

Nesika was a splendid sight in her wedding dress, which had a train ten yards long that was carried by twenty pages. On her head she wore a dazzling coronet set with the diamond image of a lioness. On his uniform Tam wore the Order of Selfless Devotion, the country's highest honor.

Tam and Nesika were the happiest couple in the land. Nesika bore her husband seven children—four princes and three princesses, all handsome, healthy, and courageous.

Nobody lives forever. A day came when the king died. Nesika became queen, and Tam her prince consort. Nesika never decided any matters of state without the advice of her husband, because whatever Tam concerned himself with turned out well.

As for Kamtsan, he felt so sorry for himself that he took to drinking. Since he remained stingy as ever, he spent his time hanging around taverns, waiting for someone to treat him. Those who had once flattered him were the first to turn away.

Even though after some time Shlimazel awoke from his sleep, he never went near Tam again. For such was the power of the wine of forgetfulness that Shlimazel didn't even remember that Tam existed. As Shlimazel had always been fond of drink and drunkards, he now attached himself to Kamtsan. Mazel, of course, continued to help Tam. Actually, Tam no longer needed Mazel, excepting once in a while. Tam had learned that good luck follows those who are diligent, honest, sincere, and helpful to others. The man who has these qualities is indeed lucky forever.

Siskiyou County Schools Library
E.S.E.A. TITLE II, PHASE TWO, 1969